LITTLE
APPLE GOAT

For Siena, Oscar, Eleanor and Tegan

Text and Illustrations © 2007 Caroline Jayne Church

This edition of *Little Apple Goat*, originally published in English in the U.K. in 2007, is published by agreement with Oxford University Press.

This edition is published by Eerdmans Books for Young Readers, an imprint of Wm. B. Eerdmans Publishing Co.

Wm. B. Eerdmans Publishing Co.
2140 Oak Industrial Dr. NE, Grand Rapids, Michigan 49505.
P.O. Box 163, Cambridge CB3 9PU U.K.

www.eerdmans.com/youngreaders

Manufactured in Singapore

07 08 09 10 11 12   8 7 6 5 4 3 2 1

Library of Congress Cataloging-in-Publication Data

Church, Caroline Jayne.
Little Apple Goat / written and illustrated by Caroline Jayne Church.
p. cm.
Summary: Little Apple Goat's love of apples, cherries, and pears helps her plant an orchard for the animals on the farm.
ISBN: 978-0-8028-5320-2 (alk. paper)
[1. Goats — Fiction. 2. Orchards — Fiction. 3. Fruit — Fiction.
4. Domestic animals — Fiction.]   I. Title.
PZ7.C466Li 2007
[E] — dc22
2006025521

Text type set in Providence
Illustrations created with collage, watercolor and black ink.

Matthew Van Zomeren, Graphic Designer

LITTLE APPLE GOAT

Written and Illustrated by
Caroline Jayne Church

Eerdmans Books for Young Readers

Grand Rapids, Michigan • Cambridge, U.K.

Down on the farm
there lived a little goat.

She was quite an ordinary goat.
Ordinary in every way.
In every way, that is, except one.

She had quite unusual eating habits.
While most goats are happy to chew
on last week's leftovers,

or Wednesday's washing,
Little Apple Goat preferred . . .

apples . . .

and pears . . .

and
cherries.

Every autumn, Little Apple Goat spent happy days in the orchard waiting for a crunchy apple, a rosy pear, or a juicy cherry to fall.

When evening came, Little Apple Goat would trot home to her meadow. And on the way she would send a shower of pits and seeds over the hedge.

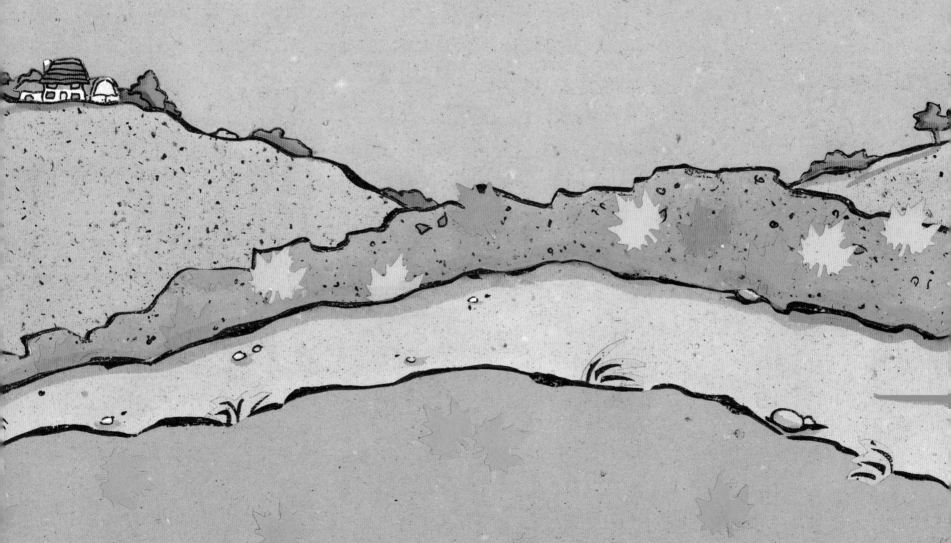

Plippety plip!

Day after day, year after year,
Little Apple Goat's pits and seeds
flew over the hedge.

On one particular autumn day,
a breeze began to blow.

The breezy afternoon
became a blustery evening . ...

The animals were very scared indeed. They huddled close together inside the barn while the wind howled all night long.

In the morning,
Little Apple Goat rushed
straight to the orchard.

The storm had toppled every single tree.
The orchard that Little Apple Goat
loved so much was gone.

All the animals were very sad when the farmer came to take the logs away.

"The farm just won't be the same without the orchard," they said.

As autumn turned to winter,
Little Apple Goat watched smoke
curl from the farmhouse chimney.

"At least the logs will keep
the farmer warm," she thought.

At last spring came.

One day Little Apple Goat noticed something bright and flowery peeking over the top of the hedge — blossoms! "Hmmm," she thought as she continued on her way.

And then one autumn, the blossoms were gone! Now fruit hung from the branches! Little Apple Goat could hardly believe it.

The animals were so happy to have a new orchard. "How did this happen? Who could have planted it?" they wondered.

But you know who, don't you?

Plippety plip! Plop!